PUFFIN BOOKS

THE MATHS WIZ

Marty Malone was a maths wizard. He loved to add, subtract and divide — the bigger the numbers the better! Marty liked to work everything out like a maths problem. But when he starts at a new school, he discovers one problem that leaves him completely stuck for an answer. Marty is useless at sports — he's always picked last for the team, and he's miserable. His teacher suggests he adds something new to the problem to help him find an answer — perhaps a friend would help? But Marty soon works out that finding a friend is not as easy as solving a maths problem.

Betsy Duffey was born in South Carolina in the United States of America. She is the daughter of the acclaimed children's writer, Betsy Byars. Betsy Duffey has written a number of books for children, and currently lives in Atlanta, Georgia, with her husband and two sons.

BETSY DUFFEY

The Maths Wiz

ILLUSTRATED BY JULIE ANDERSON

PUFFIN BOOKS

For my mother

PUFFIN BOOKS

Published by the Penguin Group
Penguin Books Ltd, 27 Wrights Lane, London W8 5TZ, England
Penguin Books USA Inc., 375 Hudson Street, New York, New York 10014, USA
Penguin Books Australia Ltd, Ringwood, Victoria, Australia
Penguin Books Canada Ltd, 10 Alcorn Avenue, Toronto, Ontario, Canada M4V 3B2
Penguin Books (NZ) Ltd, 182–190 Wairau Road, Auckland 10, New Zealand

Penguin Books Ltd, Registered Offices: Harmondsworth, Middlesex, England

First published in the United States of America by Viking Penguin Inc. 1990 under
the title *The Math Wiz* by Betsy Duffey with illustrations by Janet Wilson
First published in Great Britain by Viking 1992
Published in Puffin Books 1993
1 3 5 7 9 10 8 6 4 2

Text copyright © Betsy Duffey, 1990
Illustrations copyright © Julie Anderson, 1992
All rights reserved

The moral right of the author has been asserted

Printed in England by Clays Ltd, St Ives plc
Filmset in Linotron Palatino

Contents

The PE Problem

Marty Malone was a Maths Wizard. He could add, subtract, multiply and divide better than any other first year junior at Danville School.

When he was only four years old he did his first subtraction problem. He was sitting on the floor with his baby brother, Tad. Baby Tad was sucking hard on his bottle. His chubby hands held the bottle tightly. His eyes were almost closed.

Even way back then Marty liked to think of everything as a maths problem. He watched the baby for a while. Then he thought:

BABY + BOTTLE = QUIET BABY

Then he started wondering:

BABY − BOTTLE = ??????????

What??

Marty always said that every problem needs an answer.

So he reached over and pulled the bottle away from Baby Tad. It wasn't easy. The bottle was right in Tad's mouth. Marty pulled with all his strength, harder, harder . . . *Pop!* The bottle popped out of the baby's mouth.

BABY − BOTTLE = ?????????????

For a few seconds there was no reaction. Then Baby Tad's eyes blinked open. His face began to wrinkle. It wrinkled more and more.

Then −

Waaaaaaaaaaaaaaaaaaaaaaa!!!!!!!!!

BABY − BOTTLE = WAAAAAAAAAAAA!!!

"What are you doing in there?" called his mother from the kitchen.

"Maths, Mum," Marty answered, "just maths."

Quickly he stuck the bottle back into the baby's mouth.

All was quiet again.

By the time he started infant school he already knew how to add and subtract, to carry and borrow numbers.

The summer after infant school he did his first multiplication problem.

He had only had his guinea pigs, Plus and Minus, for a month when it started. Plus had four babies.

Everyone was delighted.

His mum brought them fresh lettuce every day from the store. His dad brought home extra newspapers from the office to put in the bottom of the cages.

Tad, who was now no longer a baby, loved to hear them squeak. Every time the fridge door opened the guinea pigs thought it was dinner time and they would start squeaking. Tad was always opening the door just to hear them.

One month later, those baby guinea pigs were grown and THEY had babies! Then another month passed and THEIR babies were grown and had babies.

Marty was thrilled. He made a chart for his bedroom wall that looked like this:

$1 \times 4 = 4$

$2 \times 4 = 8$

$4 \times 4 = 16$

By the end of the summer he had thirty
guinea pigs!

Everyone else was not thrilled.

His mother got tired of buying all that
lettuce. Thirty guinea pigs eat a lot of
lettuce.

His dad got tired of bringing home newspapers.

Everyone got tired of the *squeak, squeak, squeak*.

The multiplication problem stopped when Marty's mum called the pet shop to come and pick up all the guinea pigs. Only Minus got to stay.

Marty's mum made a new family rule:

THE PEOPLE IN THIS FAMILY MUST ALWAYS OUTNUMBER THE PETS

She wrote it on a piece of paper and put it up on the fridge with a magnet.

At the bottom of the paper Marty wrote:

PEOPLE > PETS

Marty always thought that there was no problem too big or too long for him to solve.

He had a poster taped over his desk in

his bedroom. He made it himself with poster board and markers. It said:

MATHS WIZ AT WORK

NO PROBLEM TOO BIG

NO PROBLEM TOO LONG

But now Marty had a problem that seemed too big for him to solve. A problem that was making his life miserable.

He called it the PE Problem. He thought of it like this:

MATHS WIZ $+$ PE $=$ MISERY

Pick Me!!!

Marty had only been at Danville School for two weeks. Two weeks doesn't seem like a very long time if you are at the beach or on winter holidays, but the first two weeks at a new school can seem like a long, long time. It did to Marty.

It was long enough for Marty to find out two things that would cause his PE Problem. The first was that all first year juniors had to take sports lessons, called PE at Danville School. The second thing was that Marty Malone was the worst child in the class.

Being good at maths did not prepare you for everything in the world. Being good at maths did not prepare you for PE.

*

Marty sat at the desk in his bedroom. He closed the door so that Tad would not come in and bother him.

Tad loved to sneak into his room and break his pencils. He would take them one by one and press the point down hard on the table until, *crack*, the pencil would break. Then he would laugh.

Marty did not think it was at all funny.

He was supposed to be doing his homework but he kept thinking about his problem, the PE Problem.

What made PE such a problem?

He looked round his room. Anyone could look at this room and tell that Marty did not like sports. There were no golden football or basketball trophies on his shelves. There were no rounders pennants tacked up on his walls. No balls, bats or rackets were scattered across his floor.

So, Marty didn't like sports.

That had never been a problem at Marty's old school. He had liked gym class at his old school just fine. You didn't have to like sports or even be good at sports to have fun playing games with the other kids. Sports were fun at his old school.

Things were different at Danville School. Mr McMillian, the PE teacher at Danville School, had different ideas about sport. To him sports were not games for having fun, sports were serious business.

Worst of all was something that Mr McMillian called:

"CHOOSING TEAMS"

At the beginning of each class he picked two captains. He went down a list of the class alphabetically. Each day the next two on the list would be the Captains of the Day.

Everybody would line up on a black line on the gym floor, and the captains would take turns picking out the children they wanted to have on their teams.

First one captain would choose somebody, then the other captain would choose, until everyone was chosen.

Those who were good at sports were always chosen first. Those who had lots of friends were always chosen next.

Every day for two weeks Marty had been
chosen last.

Being chosen last at PE was the worst
thing about Danville School.

Marty put his head down on his desk.
He remembered the PE lesson that
morning. It still hurt his feelings to think
about it.

As usual, the class began with "choosing teams".

Bob Cheatham was the captain of the red team. "I choose Tom Ballan!" he said importantly.

Big surprise, thought Marty. Tom Ballan was great at sports.

"I choose Tipper Grant," the blue team captain called out.

Tipper had lots of friends.

Marty's shoulders sagged. He looked down at a crack on the gym floor.

One by one the children were chosen. As their names were called they ran forward excitedly to the red or the blue team.

When they got to their team they clapped hands in a high five with the other players.

"All right!!!!" they yelled as they clapped.

20

As the children were chosen Marty tried to think about something else. He practised addition in his head.

$2+2 = 4 \ldots 4+4 = 8$.

It didn't work.

He could only think about the teams. A silent prayer kept calling in his head. *Pick me. Pick me.*

"Susie Bartow," the red captain called.

$8+8 = 16 \ldots$ *Pick me. Pick me*, his brain said.

"Randy Sims."

Pick me. Pick me.

"Julie Jackson."

Pick meeeeeeee!!!!

Slowly the picking went on and on. Still Marty stood on the line. Finally only two kids were left.

Marty looked up from the floor to sneak a peek at the other kid – Billy Beason.

Billy was in the highest maths group

with Marty. But in PE – well, in PE Billy
missed the ball when he batted at softball
and stumbled when he tried to run fast.

Billy was probably the second worst boy
in PE. Before Marty had started school two
weeks ago Billy had probably been the
WORST boy in PE.

Billy was looking down at his shoes, too.
He was used to being chosen last.

"Billy Beason," Bob called. He rolled his eyes up to the ceiling.

Billy began walking slowly towards the red team. The teams were already lining up at the volleyball net. Marty noticed that no one held up their hand for Billy to clap.

Being good at maths didn't get you far in PE, Marty had thought as he headed for the blue team.

*

Crack!

Uh-oh! Tad was at the pencils again. Marty jumped up from his desk and grabbed his pencil box. He pushed Tad out of the room. He had work to do. He closed the door and locked it this time.

He took out a blank sheet of notebook paper and put it on his desk.

The fresh white paper gave him hope.

He looked up at the sign over his desk.

NO PROBLEM TOO BIG

He could figure this one out!
At the top of the paper he wrote:

THE PE PROBLEM

Then he wrote:

MATHS WIZ + PE = MISERY

He chewed on the eraser of his pencil for a minute as he looked at the paper. Then he wrote:

MATHS WIZ − PE = ???????

He had to get out of PE.
But how?
He drew a circle around the letters PE. Under it he wrote:

HOW TO GET OUT OF PE

He chewed on his eraser some more.
Suddenly he had a plan.
A plan that would get him out of PE.
In big black letters he wrote two words:

ACE BANDAGE

Then for the first time in two weeks he smiled.

The Ace
Bandage Plan

Beep . . . Beep . . . Beep . . . Beep . . .

It was morning.

Marty reached over without getting out of bed and pushed the black button on top of his alarm clock. The beeping stopped.

He rested his head back on the pillow without opening his eyes. For a moment he imagined that he was back in his old bedroom before the move.

"Marty! . . . Marty!"

He imagined that he could hear his best friend from his old school, Jimmy, calling him to come outside and play.

"Marty! . . . Marty! Get up, Marty!"

It wasn't Jimmy. It was his mother! He pulled the covers over his head. She had ruined his daydream.

"Marty, get up for school!"

School!

Marty had almost forgotten his plan. He reached under his pillow and found the folded piece of notebook paper. He brought it out from under his pillow and sat up.

He held it tightly in his hand for a moment and then unfolded it.

He knew exactly what it said. But it gave him courage to see it again in writing.

HOW TO GET OUT OF PE
ACE BANDAGE

Marty got dressed in a hurry. He made his bed, brushed his teeth, and gathered up his homework and put it into his school bag. Then he made his move.

He ran into his parents' room and opened his father's sock drawer.

There it was, the Ace bandage.

His dad had sprained his ankle once on a hiking trip. Marty's mum had bought the Ace bandage for him at a chemist.

Marty remembered how he had put it on. The bandage was a long, brown, stretchy piece of cloth. His dad had wrapped it round and round his ankle – about twenty times. Then he had fastened it with two special clips to keep it from coming undone. It had been smooth and tight on his leg.

Marty poked the Ace bandage box into his school bag and headed downstairs.

Mission accomplished!

If he put the bandage on his leg then everyone would think that he had a sprained leg and he would not have to go to PE.

He could just imagine it:

Marty would come limping into the gym.

Everyone would drop their balls and rackets and come running over to him.

Slowly he would roll up the leg of his jeans and the Ace bandage would be wrapped tightly and smoothly around his leg.

"Ooooooooooooooooooooo!" they would say together.

The sports teacher would come hurrying over, filled with concern.

"Here, son," he would say, "lean on me. Come and sit down. No need for you to take PE today."

"It's nothing," Marty would say, waving them away.

"It's . . ."

"Marty!" his mum called again from the kitchen. "Come on down. You don't want to be late for school, do you?"

"No, Mum. I don't want to be late for school!" Marty answered as he ran down the stairs. And for once it was true.

Chubby Bubby Big Wad Chewing Gum

When Marty got to school he went straight to the boys' cloakroom. No one else was there. Everyone else was hurrying to class. The last bell was about to ring. He didn't have much time.

He took the bandage out of the box and unwound it. It was a lot longer than he had remembered.

He pulled up the leg of his jeans and tried to wind the bandage around his leg. It kept getting tangled. Finally he got it on.

It didn't look as smooth and tight as it had on his father's ankle. It looked bumpy and loose.

He looked in the box for the special clips. It was empty.

NO CLIPS!

He turned it over and shook it. He felt in every corner of the box. There were no clips in the box.

Marty didn't know quite what to do. He had got this far. He didn't want to give up now.

He checked his pocket – two five-pence pieces, one stone, one pencil stub, and one stick of Chubby Bubby Big Wad Chewing Gum.

He picked out the chewing gum.

Perfect!

He put the piece of chewing gum into his mouth and began to chew it. When it was nice and soft he stuck it on the end of the bandage. Then he stuck the end of the bandage down with the chewing gum.

Marty patted the bandage a few times to try to smooth it out.

He frowned. It did not feel very tight.

He stopped and thought for a second.

Maybe he should put the bandage back and forget the whole plan.

Brinnngggg!

The last bell!

No time left to change his mind. The bandage would have to do.

Carefully, he pulled the leg of his jeans back down over the bandage and hurried on to the first lesson.

*

Marty stayed in his seat all morning. He was afraid if he moved his leg the bandage would come undone.

He could feel it slip a little every time he moved.

He didn't go to the water fountain. He didn't go to the boys' toilets at break time. He didn't even go to the pencil sharpener once.

Finally the bell rang for PE. Marty made his way down the hall. He tried to walk with his leg stiff.

Step . . . Thump . . . Step . . . Thump.

He kept looking down to check the bandage. It was already down round his foot like a sock. It didn't feel at all tight.

It was so loose that Marty could not feel it at all. It sure wouldn't convince Mr McMillian if it got any lower.

Step . . . Thump . . . Step . . . Thump.

He looked down the hall. He was almost

at the gym. Just a little farther.

Step . . . Thump. Almost there.

He glanced down to check the bandage again.

Marty stopped and stared down at his leg. He didn't want to believe what he saw.

There was a long brown tail coming out from the bottom of his jeans. On the end of the tail was the giant wad of Chubby Bubby Big Wad Chewing Gum!

What should he do?

Should he stop and try to pick up the bandage or try to make it to the gym? If he could get to the gym maybe he could fix it before anyone noticed.

He decided to keep on walking. He didn't have far to go. He hoped no one would step on the gum.

Step . . . Thump . . . Step . . . Thump.

He walked a little faster.

He looked down the hall to see how much farther he had to go.

Uh-oh! Down the hall, coming right towards him, was Mr Hardeman, the head teacher. Mr Hardeman was looking right at him.

He tried to make his face look as normal as possible. He tried to walk as normally as possible. He tried not to look like a boy with a long brown tail coming out of his jeans leg.

Mr Hardeman was a strict head teacher. He would not think it was very funny.

As Marty watched, Mr Hardeman came closer . . . closer . . . closer . . .

Mr Hardeman nodded as he passed Marty without looking down.

Whewwww!

He didn't notice the bandage!

Marty sighed with relief. All clear!

He stopped for a few seconds and leaned back against the wall of the hall to catch his breath.

He had made it past Mr Hardeman. Now he was almost at the gym door.

He stopped and looked down one more time to check his bandage.

At the bottom of his trouser leg he could see his bare ankle. He looked closer.

Double Uh-oh! No bandage!

He pulled up his trouser leg and looked one more time. He stared at his bare leg. The bandage was gone.

Marty felt sick. He decided that he'd better find the bandage and pick it up before someone stepped on the chewing gum.

He turned round and looked down the hall to find it.

No bandage.

Where did it go?

Marty saw something moving on the floor at the end of the hall.

Something long and brown.

Triple Uh-oh!

The long brown something was following along behind Mr Hardeman.

He could no longer see the Chubby Bubby Big Wad Chewing Gum. It was stuck to the bottom of Mr Hardeman's shoe!

Mr Hardeman must have stepped on the gum. The Ace bandage was still stuck to

the chewing gum, trailing behind the head
teacher like a long tail.

He could see the other children in the
hall turning to look at Mr Hardeman as he
passed them. Some of them giggled.

Mr Hardeman nodded to each child as
he passed.

Marty shook his head. Boy, would he be

mad later when he saw what had been following him. Boy, would he be mad at Marty if he found out who did it.

Marty felt even sicker.

He did not look back again.

Before he went into the gym he pulled his piece of notebook paper out of his pocket and drew a dark black line through the words:

ACE BANDAGE

Then he started into the gym for PE.

His plan had failed.

He was not going to get out of PE today.

Captains of the Day

Tweeeeeeeeet!! Mr McMillian blew his whistle.

Marty stopped at the door to the gym. He still felt sick. His stomach hurt and his palms were cold and sweaty.

The other children pushed past him as if he were invisible.

He had seen a film once about an invisible man. In the film the man could do wonderful things because people could not see him. He surprised bank robbers at a hold-up. He listened in unseen on the plans of gangsters and stopped their crimes.

After the film Marty thought about how much fun it would be to be invisible. Now, after two weeks of feeling invisible at

Danville School he realized how wrong he was.

He smoothed down his T-shirt and put his hands in his pockets. He had worn his favourite T-shirt today to give him courage.

It was bright blue covered with white numbers. The numbers made a long problem. The problem started at the front of the shirt: $2{,}345 + 4{,}563 - 3{,}678 + 9{,}561 - 2{,}890$ . . . The numbers went on and on all over the shirt. At the bottom of the back of the shirt was an = sign but no answer.

One night Marty had worked out the problem. It had taken him two hours to figure it out. 3,742 was the answer. Only a Maths Wiz could do a problem like that!

"Move *it*! Move *it*!" the sports teacher called out to the children.

The sports teacher used to be in the army. He still acted like a drill sergeant. He rocked back and forth on his heels and tried to suck in his stomach.

The children began to line up on the long black line that ran down the side of the basketball court.

PE was serious business.

Kate Ellen Johnson pushed Marty with her elbow as she passed by. Kate Ellen was always in a hurry. When she walked she moved her arms back and forth as if she were pushing people out of the way.

Sally Long followed her like a shadow.

"Sir, Sir . . . Sir," Kate Ellen called out in a high, squeaky voice.

"Sir, isn't it our turn to be Captains of the Day? See, we're up to the *J*s. Johnson should be next."

The sports teacher gave her a tired look and rocked back and forth on his heels some more.

Kate Ellen wrinkled her nose up as if she smelled something awful. She was always doing that. Marty hated it. It always made him feel like the something awful was him.

"See, we were up to Jenkins yesterday. Now we should be up to Johnson."

The sports teacher gave Kate Ellen a long, hard look.

"And then comes *L* for Long," said Sally like an echo.

"Move *it*, girls," he said loudly. "Line up now or there won't be any teams today – there will be LAPS to run."

Kate Ellen and Sally hurried towards the black line.

The sports teacher turned to face the other children. Some were not yet lined up.

"I SAID there will be LAPS to run," he said in a loud voice. "Would anyone like to run some LAPS today?"

At the sound of the word *laps* the class began to line up quickly. Nobody liked to

run laps. Marty hurried over to his place
on the line.

Why would anyone WANT to be
Captain of the Day, Marty wondered. He
could think of nothing worse than
standing up in front of the class picking
out the ones to be on his team.

He could just imagine it.

They would all be lined up on the black
line.

The sports teacher would call out, "Captain of the Day, MARTY MALONE."

Marty would step forward from the black line and would call out his first choice.

"Tom Ballan," he would say.

"No, thanks!" Tom Ballan would say and he would head towards the other team.

"Tipper Grant," Marty would say.

"No, thanks!" Tipper would say and she would go to the other team, too.

Pretty soon the entire class would be on the other team.

It would be like one long subtraction problem. One by one each kid would be subtracted until there was only Marty left.

He would be left alone on the blue team.

Being Captain of the Day might even be worse than being chosen last.

If they were up to the Ls, then the Ms were next. Malone started with M. Tomorrow would be Marty's turn to be Captain of the Day.

He decided to be absent tomorrow.

Tweeeeeeet!

Uh-oh! PE was starting.

"Volleyball! Choose teams!" called the sports teacher.

Double Uh-oh! Marty hated volleyball.

"Captains of the Day . . . Kate Ellen Johnson and Sally Long."

Triple Uh-oh! thought Marty.

He settled in to be chosen last.

The teams were chosen. Last again!

Marty decided that today he would try as hard as he could. Today he would be good at PE.

The teams lined up and faced each other at the volleyball net. They took turns bouncing the ball back and forth over the net.

The sports teacher blew his whistle and the game began. Everyone was serious now. The ball went back and forth across the net and everybody tried hard not to miss it when it came to them.

Marty watched the ball closely. If it came to him he would be ready.

Finally the ball came high over the net right towards Marty. His big chance. His chance to get noticed.

"Get it, Marty!" someone called. They were cheering for him!

"Go, Marty!" He wouldn't let them down. This time he would hit the ball back over the net.

The ball seemed like it moved in slow motion as it made its way down.

Marty reached up his hands . . .

Kerthump!!

The ball hit Marty right on the top of his head.

Marty looked at his hands in disbelief. How could they have failed him?

The sports teacher groaned. The other team made a point.

Marty felt his face turn red. He moved to the back of the volleyball court. He was no longer interested in the game.

It was hopeless.

He kept his eyes on the floor and hoped that the ball would not come to him again.

When he looked up he could see Billy Beason on the other team staring at him.

He must think I'm a real wally, thought Marty.

He wished PE would be over. He looked up at the clock on the wall of the gym. In fifteen minutes he would be in Miss Williams's maths class.

Miss Williams was the one good thing about Danville School. Her class was wonderful.

It had problems, problems and more problems. And Marty was an expert at solving problems.

What was the solution to the PE Problem? Marty wondered.

MATHS WIZ + PE = MISERY

There had to be a way to make that problem come out differently.

Somehow, some way, today during the maths lesson he would solve the PE Problem.

But first he had to make it through PE.

Boy + Good at Maths
= ????

Tweeeeeeeet!

Wow. He was terrific.

If Marty was the worst person in PE, Tom Ballan was the best.

He was tall and was the only one in the class with muscles. He wore his T-shirt sleeves rolled up to the shoulders and was

"Take five!" yelled the sports teacher.

That was his way of saying, "Take a water break."

Some of the children went to the drinking fountain. Some of the others sat down on the benches and talked to each other.

Marty did not go with them. He was left alone.

At the other end of the gym Marty could see Tom Ballan. He stood out from the others, bouncing the volleyball on his knee. First one knee – then the other – then up to his head – then knee, elbow, head.

always stretching. Now he stretched out his arm and flexed it up. As he flexed his arm a real muscle bumped up.

Marty looked down at his own arm. He did not bend it up and flex it. He knew there would be no bump on his arm.

Boys with muscles were good at sports. Tom Ballan was always chosen first for volleyball and softball teams.

Marty thought of it like a maths problem.

BOY + MUSCLES = GOOD AT SPORTS

He thought of it another way:

BOY + GOOD AT SPORTS = ???

What?

FRIENDS, he decided.

BOY + GOOD AT SPORTS = FRIENDS

What was so special about sports anyway?

Why couldn't something HE was good at be considered special – like maths?

Marty sighed. He tried to make it into a problem:

BOY + GOOD AT MATHS = ????

He couldn't finish the problem.

He didn't think the answer was FRIENDS. But what was it??? He tried again.

BOY + GOOD AT MATHS = 'A'S ON REPORTS

'A's on reports sure were nice but right now he sure would like the answer to be *friends*, too.

If you can throw a ball or run fast, crowds of people cheer and go wild over you. You just didn't see crowds of people going wild over maths, did you?

But . . . what if they did????

He could just imagine it.

The gym would be filled with hundreds of cheering children. In front of a large blackboard would be Marty, his blue uniform shiny under the bright lights. Beside him in a red uniform, the challenger.

Tweeet! The teacher would blow his whistle and Marty and the challenger would begin to add long columns of numbers.

"Go, Marty!" someone would call out just like they had in the volleyball game. But this time would not be like the volleyball game. This time he could do it.

Everybody would cheer him on as he added the long columns of numbers.

"MATHS WIZ!!!!!"

"MATHS WIZ!!!!!"

"MATHS . . ."

Tweeeeeeeet!

The sports teacher's whistle interrupted his daydream.

"That's it for today! Move on out!"

PE was over.

Marty began to move towards the door with the other kids.

He had survived another day of PE.

"Move it! Move it!" the sports teacher called out, louder this time. "I SAID, move on out!"

"With pleasure!" Marty said softly to himself and he headed out of the gym door to maths class.

Triple Uh-Oh

The first year juniors were divided up for maths. Those who were the best at maths went to Miss Williams's room. The others went to different rooms.

Marty took a seat in the back row and began to organize his pencils. He had three pencils – all with sharp points. If one broke, he would always have a spare.

Miss Williams was passing out white sheets of paper. She placed the papers face down on the children's desks.

"We'll start the class with a time test," she announced. "Subtraction."

"Oh, no!" Marty heard someone whisper.

Marty smiled. He loved time tests. What could be more fun than a whole page of problems just waiting to be solved?

Miss Williams finished handing out the tests. She reached in her desk and pulled out a small silver stopwatch.

"You will have ten minutes." She held up the watch.

"Ready . . . BEGIN!" she called out as she pushed the button on the top of the stopwatch.

Quickly the children turned over their papers and began to work out the problems. If they finished all the problems before the ten minutes was over, they raised their hands.

Marty finished all his problems in only four minutes. His hand shot up.

Miss Williams hurried over to his desk.

"Very good, Marty," she whispered as she wrote *4 min. 20 sec.* on the bottom of his paper.

She smiled at him.

"You may work in your exercise book until the others finish."

Marty looked round the room. No one else was finished. Marty had five more minutes to wait before the test would be over.

He took out his exercise book. He opened it but he did not work in it. Instead he pulled his piece of notebook paper out

of his pocket, the PE Problem. He put it
inside his exercise book so it would look
like he was working in his exercise book.

He looked at the problem:

MATHS WIZ + PE = MISERY

He chewed on the eraser of his pencil for
a few seconds as he looked at the paper.
Then he wrote:

CHANGE THE PROBLEM!!

Last week in maths class they learned that if you change any part of a problem, the answer changes, too. In the PE Problem the answer was misery. Marty really wanted to change that answer. But what could he change in the problem?

He looked at the first part – MATHS WIZ. Maths Wiz was Marty. He was good in maths. He had tried as hard as he could to be good at volleyball. He just was not good in PE. He really couldn't change that.

He wrote beside MATHS WIZ: CAN'T CHANGE THIS and drew a line to where the problem said MATHS WIZ.

He looked at the next part – PE. Marty had already tried to get out of PE. All first year juniors had to take PE. He shook his head and wrote: CAN'T CHANGE THIS and drew a line to PE.

He chewed on his eraser some more.

*

"Marty . . . Marty Malone . . ."

Uh-oh! Back to maths class.

"Did you hear me, Marty?"

Double Uh-oh! Miss Williams did not
look happy.

"Uh, yes," said Marty.

"Then could you please give us the next
answer?"

"Answer??" Marty said. They were

checking the answers on the time test. He did not even know what problem they were on.

He looked down at his test paper, helplessly.

"Go ahead, Marty," Miss Williams said. "We're waiting."

Miss Williams did not sound pleased. She tapped her foot.

Tap . . . Tap . . . Tap . . .

Marty did not look up from his paper.

The class was silent. The only sound was the sound of Miss Williams's foot.

Tap . . . Tap . . . Tap . . .

"I know, Miss Williams!" a high, squeaky voice called out.

It was Kate Ellen, waving her hand wildly in the air. "I know, it's 68!"

"Kate Ellen!" Miss Williams said, turning to the other side of the room. "We do not answer out of turn!"

"Sorry," she said, sounding not one bit
sorry.

Kate Ellen looked directly at Marty and
wrinkled her nose and smiled.

She had saved him!

Marty began to like the way she
wrinkled her nose.

He quickly shuffled his PE Problem
under his test so that Miss Williams would
not see it.

He looked down at his test and looked for the answer that was 68. Now he knew right where they were checking.

He hoped that Miss Williams would call on him again.

He raised his hand but she did not give him a second chance.

"Tom Ballan, could you give us the answer to the last problem?"

There was a long silence.

"234?" Tom answered.

"The correct answer is 334," Miss Williams said.

Someone giggled. Tom looked down at his paper and turned red.

Tom looked like he felt as bad as Marty had felt when he missed the volleyball in PE.

Miss Williams began to collect the papers.

"You may work in your exercise books

until the bell rings. Work the page numbers written on the board," she said as she walked down each row of desks picking up the test papers.

When she got to Marty's desk she reached down and picked up his test paper.

This time she did not smile.

Marty looked down at the spot where his test paper had been. The PE Problem had been under the test paper.

BOTH were gone.

Triple Uh-oh!

Miss Williams had the PE Problem!

A Note to Marty

Marty worked out a few problems in his exercise book. He tried to concentrate on his work but he couldn't.

He looked around the room.

Billy Beason was staring at him again.

He wondered why. He looked down to be sure his zipper was zipped. He licked his hand and smoothed down his cowlick.

Billy still stared.

He must think I'm a real wally, Marty thought again.

Marty looked up to the front of the room where Miss Williams was correcting the maths tests.

When she came to his she would know all about his PE Problem. Worse than that she would know about the Ace bandage.

By now he was sure that Mr Hardeman had found out about the Ace bandage on his shoe. He would be looking for the kid who did that to him. He would be looking for Marty.

Miss Williams would probably send him to the head teacher's office.

He tried to work out a few more problems.

Then he put his head down on his desk and closed his eyes.

"Psssst," someone hissed from the other side of the room.

"Pssssst!"

He looked up and saw a note being passed. He wondered who the note was for.

The class was good at note passing.

Kate Ellen had the note. She pretended to yawn. When she stretched out her arm she dropped the note on Susie Bartow's desk.

Susie tapped the back of Julie Jackson's neck with the note. Julie reached back and scratched her neck and took the note.

Julie put the note in her shoe and lifted her foot up high beside Bob Cheatham's desk.

Bob took the note and pulled a large rubber band out of his pocket. He put the rubber band around the note and pulled it back like a sling-shot. Then – *whooosh* – he shot the note directly on to Marty's desk.

Everyone giggled. Miss Williams looked up quickly from her desk.

"Class, is there a problem?" she asked.

"No, Miss Williams," someone answered.

"Then let's get on with our work," she said.

Marty waited a minute until Miss Williams looked back down at the papers on her desk. Then he looked at the note.

To: Marty was written on the front of the note.

Who could have sent him a note? he wondered.

He began to unfold the note.

Bbbrrrinnnnnggggg!!

The bell rang. School was over.

Miss Williams looked up from her desk.

Marty quickly stuck the note in his back pocket. He did not want to get into any MORE trouble with Miss Williams.

The note would have to wait.

3,742

The other children picked up their books and headed towards the door.

Miss Williams stood at the door and handed back the time tests as each one left.

Marty stayed in his seat. He couldn't decide. Should he wait until everyone left and then go up and get his papers from Miss Williams? Or should he try to slip on through with them?

He watched as each one got back their test. When they saw their grades some of them groaned. He watched Billy get his test back. Billy looked at his paper and smiled. Then Billy stopped just outside the door and looked back like he was waiting for someone.

Marty sighed. He wished that Billy was

waiting for HIM but he knew it wasn't possible. Billy thought he was a wally.

He decided not to go out until all the others were gone. He put his head down on his desk until he heard the last kid leave the room.

When he looked up Billy was gone.

Marty got up and moved slowly to the door.

Without saying a word, Miss Williams handed him his papers. He could tell by the way it felt that it was more than one

paper. He could tell that it was more than two papers. It felt like about three papers.

Marty moved like a zombie through the door and headed slowly towards home.

He was afraid to look at the papers. He carried them tightly in his fist, slightly crumpled.

He decided that one of the papers must be a note to his parents. He could just imagine what it said.

Dear Mr and Mrs Malone,

Your son has been in a little trouble today. He attached an Ace bandage to the head teacher's shoe with a wad of Chubby Bubby Big Wad Chewing Gum.

It was true. He looked down at the pavement. The pavement blurred.

His parents would have to sign the note and send it back.

They would not be happy about this.

Usually when Marty got home from school he ran right into the kitchen for a snack. But today he wasn't at all hungry. Today he went straight upstairs to his room.

He put the papers on his desk and smoothed them out. He sat down.

Then he took a deep breath and looked down at the top paper.

It was his time test.

A + was written on the top line.

Miss Williams must not be too *mad,* thought Marty, *if she gave me an* A +. He began to feel a little better.

He moved the test paper to the side and stared down at the next page. It was the PE Problem, but something had been added to it.

Miss Williams had corrected it just like she corrected all his maths papers!

Under the problem she had written in
red ink:

Another way to change the answer to a
problem is to add something new to the
problem.

Then she wrote:

MATHS WIZ + PE + A FRIEND = ??????

A friend?

A friend would make PE a lot better.
Marty wished that adding a friend to his
life was as easy as writing it down on a
piece of notebook paper. It wasn't that
easy!

He crumpled the paper into a ball and

threw it into his waste-paper basket. The PE
Problem had caused him enough trouble.

That left one more sheet of paper from
Miss Williams. It was not a note to his
parents.

It was blue and was printed with big
block letters.

Marty read it. Then he smiled.

MATHS CLUB PICNIC
WHEN: WEDNESDAY AFTER SCHOOL
WHERE: PLAYING FIELD
WHO: ALL MEMBERS AND
ALL STUDENTS WHO LIKE MATHS
WHAT TO BRING: PAPER AND PENCILS

At the bottom of the page in red ink Miss
Williams had written:

The perfect place for a Maths Wiz
to find a friend!

Marty sat at his desk and thought about the maths club picnic. Lots of kids would be there – kids who liked maths like Marty.

He decided he would go.

Suddenly Marty felt hungry. As he headed downstairs to the kitchen for his snack, he remembered his note.

He sat down on the bottom step and took it out of his pocket. He quickly unfolded it.

It was the shortest note that Marty had ever seen. It had no words at all, only a number.

3,742

He stared at the note for a few seconds. Then he remembered –

His T-shirt!

3,742 was the answer to the problem on his T-shirt! He turned the paper over.

From: Billy, it said on the back.

Billy Beason! That's why Billy had been

staring at him all day. He was staring at the problem on Marty's T-shirt.

Maybe Billy didn't think he was a wally.

Maybe Billy had been waiting for HIM outside the door after maths class.

Marty wondered if Billy would be at the maths club picnic.

Marty smiled again.

BOY + GOOD AT MATHS = FRIENDS

Maybe it could be true after all.

The Solution

The next day Marty ran all the way to school. Today he would solve the PE Problem!

He hurried down the hall to his classroom. Ahead he could see the door to Mr Hardeman's office. He walked a little slower.

He remembered the Ace bandage. He remembered Mr Hardeman walking down the hall with the Ace bandage attached to his shoe. He remembered the note to his parents that he had imagined yesterday.

Your son has been in a little trouble today . . .

Was he in trouble?

Was Mr Hardeman looking for him?

What had happened to the Ace
bandage?

As Marty passed the door to the head
teacher's office, he began to tiptoe. He
didn't want to run into Mr Hardeman
today.

Bang!

The door flew open.

Mr Hardeman!!!! Marty froze.

"Good morning, Marty," Mr Hardeman
said. He nodded and hurried past Marty.

He didn't look at all mad!

He must not know!

Before the door could close again a hand reached out and put a waste-paper basket into the hall for the morning collection.

Marty looked down at the pile of rubbish in the waste-paper basket and smiled. Right on top was something long and brown and stretchy – the Ace bandage.

Mr Hardeman must not be looking for him if he was throwing away the evidence!

Marty started to pick up the Ace bandage, then he changed his mind. He gave it one farewell glance and headed down the hall to class.

He wouldn't be needing it any more.

The lesson began.

All morning Marty watched the clock.

The bell for PE rang and for the first time since he started Danville School the sound of the PE bell did not make Marty feel sick. He didn't mind going to PE.

He hurried to the gym.

Tweeeeettttttt!

Today the sound of the sports teacher's whistle didn't bother Marty.

"Softball – choose teams," called the sports teacher.

Today "choosing teams" didn't bother Marty.

"Captains of the Day . . . Sam Miller and Marty Malone."

Even being Captain of the Day didn't bother Marty.

He hurried forward from the black line to choose his team. He didn't feel at all invisible.

He looked down the line at the kids in his class: Kate Ellen, Tom, Billy, Sally and all the others.

For the first time he saw them as

different people, not just as a group.

Some were good in PE, others good in art. Some were good in maths, others in writing. Every one of them was different. Every one of them was strong in some ways and not so strong in other ways just like Marty.

Today he was glad that he was good in maths. Maths was what he liked. Maths was what made him happy. So what if he was not good in PE? Everyone was not good at everything.

He stood tall and got ready to call out his first choice for the red team.

Tom Ballan and Tipper Grant leaned forward, ready to be called.

"I choose . . ." Marty said clearly and proudly . . .

"Billy Beason."

Billy looked up at Marty. His mouth dropped open in surprise. He had NEVER

been chosen first in PE.

His face broke into a big grin as he ran forward from the black line.

Smack!! went his hand against Marty's as they gave each other the high five. And together they broke into a yell –

"All right!!!!!!!"

MATHS WIZ + PE + A FRIEND =
ALL RIGHT!!!!!!!!